This Winter

A *Heartstopper* novella

Alice Oseman

HarperCollins *Children's Books*

NICK AND CHARLIE

THIS WINTER

RADIO SILENCE

LOVELESS

HEARTSTOPPER

I WAS BORN FOR THIS

SOLITAIRE

HEARTSTOPPER

Books by Alice Oseman

SOLITAIRE

RADIO SILENCE

I WAS BORN FOR THIS

LOVELESS
WINNER OF THE YA BOOK PRIZE 2021

Novellas by Alice Oseman

NICK AND CHARLIE

THIS WINTER

Graphic novels by Alice Oseman

HEARTSTOPPER VOLUME 1

HEARTSTOPPER VOLUME 2

HEARTSTOPPER VOLUME 3

HEARTSTOPPER VOLUME 4

'It is evident by this,' added Jane, 'that he comes back no more this winter.'

Pride and Prejudice, Jane Austen

Victoria Annabel Spring,
Age 16

Tori

I wake up two hours after I fall asleep. The amount of sleep I get on Christmas Eve seems to be decreasing each year, probably because my average falling-asleep time gets steadily later due to my rather worrying Internet addiction. Maybe, eventually, I'll just stop sleeping altogether and become a vampire. I'd be good at that.

Not gonna bother complaining about my sleeping pattern right now though, because it's Christmas and this is the one day of the year when I should at least try not to complain about anything. This is hard when your seven-year-old brother is hitting you in the face with a pillow at six o'clock in the morning.

I say something along the lines of 'nooooo' and retreat under my duvet, but this doesn't stop Oliver from following, tearing back the covers and crawling on to my bed.

'*Tori*,' he whispers. 'It's *Christmas*.'

'Mm.'

'Are you awake?'

'No.'

'You are!'

'No.'

'*Tori*.'

'Oliver. . . go wake Charlie up.'

'Mum said I wasn't allowed.' He starts ruffling my hair. 'Toriiiiiiii—'

'*Ugh*.' I roll over and open my eyes. Oliver is

completely under the covers, looking at me, wriggling with excitement, his hair sticking up on end like a dandelion. Charlie and I have discussed at length how it's possible for Oliver to be related to us, since he's the literal embodiment of joy and we're both miserable fucks. We concluded that he must have got all the happy genes.

Oliver has a Christmas card in his hands.

'Why do you have a—'

He opens the card and a disgustingly cheerful version of 'We Wish You a Merry Christmas' begins to play right into my ear.

I groan and shove Oliver off the bed with one hand. He rolls on to the floor and bursts into giggles.

'So annoying,' I mutter, before sitting up and turning on my bedside lamp, resulting in a shriek of 'YAY!' from Oliver. He begins to wander around my room, opening and closing the card so it repeats the first two notes over and over again.

Christmas is okay at our house. It's chilled. Quiet. Dad calls it a Spring Christmas, which he thinks is hilarious. We open presents when we wake up, then family come over for Christmas dinner and stay until late, and that's it. I play video games with my brothers and cousins, Dad always gets drunk, my Spanish grandfather (Dad's dad) has an argument with my English grandfather (Mum's dad) – truly wonderful stuff.

But it's not exactly a normal Christmas Day this year.

My fifteen-year-old brother, Charlie, has an eating disorder. Anorexia. He's had it for a long time, but it's been particularly bad these past few months, and the stress of it caused him to have a self-harm relapse too back in October. He lived away from home for a few weeks at a psychiatric ward that specifically cares for teenagers who have eating disorders and it definitely helped, but it's still been rough. Obviously.

I don't really think there was a reason he got so ill. That stuff just happens, like diseases or cancer. So it's not his fault. Actually, I think it was probably my fault it got so bad. When I noticed that something was *off* with him, I didn't tell my parents and I didn't ask him what was wrong. I didn't talk to him enough. I didn't do enough.

But it's not about how I feel. It's not even about my parents. Christmas is a stressful time for people with eating disorders, since food is such a big part of the day, and I know Charlie's been feeling anxious about it. He's been stressed all week, arguing with Mum pretty much every day and shutting himself in his room.

So today is about supporting Charlie.

I pick up my phone, ignore the notifications and text Becky, my best friend.

Tori Spring

(06:16) *HAPPY CHRISTMAS. Be thankful you don't have siblings. I am tired. Oliver threw a pillow at me. Enjoy sleep. Bye.* xxxxxxxxxxxxxxx

Mum and Dad said we can't wake them up until at least 7:30. It's 6:17 now. I get up and open my curtains to find the world still dark, tinged yellow from the street lamps. I fall back into bed and put the radio on. It's playing a quiet hymn for once, instead of 'All I Want for Christmas Is You'. It's nice. Oliver is spinning around in my desk chair and a choir is singing 'Silent Night', my eyes are closing again and now Oliver's sitting in my bed with me, the musical card on a pile of clothes on the floor, it's 6:29, 6:42, 6:55 ... Oliver's pulling my hair gently, he's talking about what presents he wants and whether Father Christmas ate the biscuits we left him and I'm mumbling something, I don't know what, I'm drifting off ...

And then my bedroom door opens again.

'. . . Victoria?'

I wake up for the tenth time. It's Charlie, just visible in the dim light standing at the door in a navy Adidas sweatshirt and checked pyjama bottoms. He looks tired but he's smiling. 'You awake?'

'No,' I say. 'I'm having an out-of-body experience. I'm just my ghost.'

Charlie snorts and enters my room. I turn to Oliver, who has fallen asleep against my shoulder, and give him a little nudge with my elbow. He snaps awake and sees Charlie.

'CHARLIE'S HERE!' he yells and charges from the bed towards him, slamming into Charlie's legs and almost causing him to fall over. Charlie laughs and picks Oliver up like he's a baby, which he does at least once a day, causing him to giggle. 'Wow, you're very awake, aren't you?'

'Can we go downstairs yet?'

Charlie carries Oliver towards my bed. 'Nope, Mum said seven thirty.'

'*Arrghhhh.*' Oliver wriggles in Charlie's arms and drops down next to me, immediately snuggling under the covers, and then Charlie sits down next to him against the headboard.

'Ugh. Younger brothers are annoying,' I say, but I'm sort of grinning too. I curl up under the duvet. 'Couldn't you stay in your own beds?'

'Just doing our job,' Charlie smiles. 'Are you listening to Radio 4? What's with the church music?'

'I don't think I can deal with Mariah Carey at this time of the morning.'

Charlie laughs. 'Me neither.' Like Oliver, his hair is sticking up from his forehead. He's got purple circles under his eyes and I can't remember what he looks like without them any more. Aside from that, he looks almost his normal self, all long-limbed and gentle.

'I only slept for like two hours,' I say.

'Same,' he says, but I think his lack of sleep might be from different reasons to mine.

'How many presents does Father Christmas give you when you're seven?' asks Oliver, who's now standing up on my bed and trampling over the duvet. Charlie and I laugh.

'Seven,' says Charlie decisively. 'The same as the number of years you've been alive.'

'So . . . when I'm eighty, I'll get eighty presents?'

Charlie prods Oliver in the chest and he falls over with a wide smile. 'Only if you've been good!'

'I can't wait till I'm eighty,' says Oliver.

'Me neither,' says Charlie.

It's good that we're all back together now. It felt weird, just me and Oliver and Mum and Dad. Oliver's still too young to talk to properly, and I don't hate my parents or anything but I don't feel like I'm too friendly with them either. Mum has this thing where she avoids talking about anything even slightly deep or emotional. Dad's the same, but he makes up for it by talking about books all the time. We all get along fine, but I don't feel like we ever talk about anything important.

They still don't even like talking openly about Charlie's eating disorder, even though he's getting proper treatment now. I thought things might change; that we might start being more open about feelings and stuff.

But we're not.

'Can you imagine being a *really old man*?' Charlie says, putting on an old-man voice, and Oliver giggles, shuffling up to join us against the headboard. Charlie's smile is contagious.

They start playing I-spy. Today's going to be difficult

for everyone, but everyone has difficult days, I guess. I used to think that difficult was better than boring, but I know better now. There have been a lot of difficult days in the past few months. There have been too many difficult days.

'Happy Christmas,' says Charlie, without any warning. He leans over Oliver and rests his head on mine. I lean a little too, my head on his shoulder. The radio plays. I think the sun is rising, or it might just be the street lamps. I'm not going to think about the past few months, about Charlie and me, about all of the sadness. I'm going to block it all out. Just for today.

'Happy Christmas,' I say.

I try not to fall asleep again, but I still do, Oliver's laugh ringing in my ears.

★

It's ten to twelve and me and Charlie are still in our pyjamas, sitting on the sofa playing the new edition of

Mario Kart. It was a present for Oliver, but he's busy with the very large amount of toy tractors that people gave him.

My parents got me a new laptop and Charlie a new phone – things we both asked for. They don't really do surprise presents. And while Charlie and I have never really tried too hard with presents before now, this year I got him a Bluetooth speaker for his bedroom and he got me a laptop case with Wednesday Addams on it. I think we both know each other better than we thought we did.

'Is it me or is this version way harder than the old one?' I ask Charlie.

He attempts to swerve Baby Mario around a corner but ends up driving off a cliff instead. 'It really is. I used to actually be *good* at this.'

I drive Bowser directly into a tree and fall into last place. 'D'you think we should try Rainbow Road?'

'I dunno. I don't think my self-esteem can take the hit.'

'Wow.'

He snorts. 'Too real?'

I smirk. 'Maybe.'

'Kids?' Mum wanders into the room. She's got her Christmas dress on – a purple thing that's actually quite nice – and her hair curled. She always makes us dress up nice for Christmas, as if we're supposed to do something other than slob on the sofa for twelve hours. She raises her eyebrows at us. 'You going to get dressed soon?'

Charlie says nothing, so I say, 'Yep, in a minute.'

'Don't be too long. Everyone's arriving in half an hour.'

'Yeah, we're just gonna finish this level.'

Mum leaves. I glance at Charlie, but he hasn't looked away from the screen. I don't think they've had an argument today but I can feel one brewing. And I'm not going to lie, Mum is kind of pissing me off a little bit. She's been really snappy with Charlie since he got home, which isn't helping anyone. If she just checked in with Charlie politely – like, asked him how he's feeling today – maybe Charlie wouldn't mind actually opening up to her.

'You feeling okay about today?' I ask. I don't want to bring up Christmas dinner. Charlie and Dad made a meal plan so Charlie could feel prepared, but I read online that talking to Charlie about food and eating all the time actually makes him feel worse.

'I'm fine,' he says. I guess maybe we shouldn't talk about it.

We get to the end of the level, and then I say, 'We have to do Rainbow Road before we go get changed.'

'Really? You think you can handle that amount of absolute failure?'

'You never know. I might be good at it.'

Charlie laughs at me. 'We'll see about that.'

*

I end up wearing the only skirt that I own, which is grey, with a collared shirt and jumper. I rarely get dressed up, since I am the most unsociable person ever to grace the earth, so I take the opportunity to brush my hair, which is probably the first time I've done that this entire holiday. Ten points to me.

Family members start to arrive and Charlie and I are on 'greeting duty', which involves more hugging than I would like. First Grandma and Grandad arrive, Grandad grumbling about something to do with his car, and Grandma gives us an apologetic look. Then our Spanish grandparents arrive, having travelled from Mojácar last week to stay with Uncle Ant's family, and Charlie has a mangled conversation in Spanish with Abuelo while Nan embarks on a long lamentation on how I cut most of my hair off in the summer.

Dad's brother and his family arrive with them –
Uncle Ant and Aunt Jules, and our three cousins:
Clara, a twenty-year-old veterinary student; Esther,
who's my age; and Rosanna, a twelve-year-old who
never seems to stop talking. Then we've got Mum's
sister Aunt Wendy, several older relatives that I'm still
not sure how exactly we're related, Dad's sister Sofia
and her husband Omar and their new baby boy – the
house is pretty full. Hopefully a bit later I'll be able to
sneak off to my room for a break.

We don't see our cousins more than a few times
a year, but it has become clear to me over recent
years that they are very much unlike Charlie and me.
Mainly because they seem determined to be friendly
and fun all the time.

'Charlie, darling,' says Clara from across the Kids Table
once Christmas dinner is fully underway. Clara looks
excellent in whatever she wears and has been allowed to

attend Christmas Day in jeans, which annoys me quite a lot. She points a fork at Charlie, who's on my left. 'You need to tell us all about your new boyfriend.'

Esther perks up at this, staring at Charlie through her glasses. Esther doesn't usually talk to us as much as Clara and Rosanna, but, from what I can tell from her Twitter, there's a possibility she might not be straight and is therefore always interested in Charlie's love life, what with him being the only openly gay person in our entire family.

Charlie shuffles in his chair. He's wearing black jeans and still the navy Adidas sweatshirt, which I suddenly realise belongs to Nick. I think he chose his outfit purposefully to annoy Mum.

Clara takes a decisive mouthful of potato. 'What's his name?'

'Nick.' There's a bit of hesitation in his voice. He probably didn't expect an inquisition on top of his other issues with dinner.

'How long have you been going out?'

'Er . . . eight months.'

'Oh! Not exactly new, then!' Clara laughs.

Charlie fiddles with his sweatshirt sleeves. 'Haha . . .
no . . .'

Clara clearly can't tell that she's making Charlie
uncomfortable. Charlie keeps glancing towards where
Grandma and Grandad are sitting, making sure they
can't hear anything from our table. Charlie doesn't
want to come out to Grandma and Grandad yet
because we think they might be a bit homophobic.
Lots of old people are, unfortunately.

'And you met at school, did you?'

I wish Clara would just shut up. This isn't her
fucking business.

'Yeah.' Charlie forces a laugh. 'Did Uncle Ant tell
you all this, or . . . ?'

'Oh God, yes, you know what he's like.'

Esther watches Charlie carefully. Rosanna is trying to plait Oliver's hair, much to Oliver's irritation.

Clara continues, 'You should *totally* bring him to ours tomorrow.'

Esther meets her eye and grins. 'Oh my God, yes.'

We go to their house every year for Boxing Day, and boyfriends and girlfriends are always welcome, but it's not like me or Charlie have ever had anyone to bring before, since he only started dating Nick in April and I dislike most people.

Charlie smiles awkwardly. 'Oh, I think he's doing stuff with his family tomorrow.'

Clara pouts. 'Aw, that's a shame.' And then her piercing gaze swaps to me. 'What about you, Tori? Any lovely men in your life?'

I fight down the urge to hysterically laugh. 'Um. No. Haha. No.'

Clara does the laughing for me. 'Oh gosh, you are not missing much, I promise you that. Straight boys are the absolute worst.' She points her fork towards Oliver. 'Let's all hope that this one turns out better.'

'He might not be straight,' Esther finally pitches in. Her voice sounds startlingly like Clara's, but I think I like Esther more than Clara. We've had some okay conversations about *Doctor Who*.

'You're so right,' says Clara, leaning on one hand, gazing at Oliver like he's a newborn. 'Charlie, when did you know you were gay?'

Charlie's eyes widen in fear at the prospect of having to embark on this conversation, but thankfully, at that moment, Dad appears at the head of the table, still with his apron on over his shirt and waistcoat, and a Christmas cracker crown hanging dangerously off the top of his head. 'How's everybody doing over here?' He looks specifically at Charlie and claps him

on the shoulder. 'Everyone doing okay?'

For the first time, I have a look at Charlie's plate. He does appear to have eaten some of it, which is a very good sign, since Charlie didn't even like roast dinner that much *before* his eating disorder. But while it's good that Dad's checking in, he's also drawing everyone's attention to Charlie, which is pretty much the last thing Charlie wants.

'We're fine,' I say quickly.

Dad meets my eyes and gives me a little nod. 'All right-y. Let me know if you need any more to drink.' He wanders back to his table.

Charlie turns to me and says quietly, 'He's so *pester-y*.'

I don't really want to say it, but I do anyway. 'I think he might just be worried.'

Charlie rolls his eyes. 'Can't I just have a normal ...' But his voice dies away and he goes back to staring at his plate.

He doesn't say much more for the whole meal, which means that I have to suffer through a horrific question-and-answer session from Rosanna about all of my school friends, and then Esther wants an update on what TV shows I watch, and then Clara gets started on the whole 'so what are you thinking about for university' thing, to which my answer is simply, 'I'm not.'

Charlie keeps taking out his phone and texting under the table, which kind of starts to piss me off, but I don't really want to annoy him, as everyone else in this family is doing that already.

I manage to escape the cousin trio after dinner and sit quietly on the sofa, so I check my own phone.

Becky Allen

(11:07) *Lmaooooo I'm so glad i'm an only child.*

(11:09) *MERRY CHRISTMAS YOU INSOMNIAC*

(11:10) *Love u xxxxxxxxxxxxxx*

(12:22) *Dad got me the new Call of Duty. See you in my next life x*

(14:01) *Mum's so drunk already. Can your family adopt me?*

(14:54) *MUM IS DANCING ON A CHAIR*

(14:59) *#SaveBecky*

'How are you feeling, anyway, Charlie?'

Uncle Ant's voice snaps my attention away from my phone. Uncle Ant is very much like Clara – big on gossip, big on talking about deep things, generally very irritating. He's sitting on a chair on the other side of the room, facing Charlie, who's next to me on the sofa.

'Er . . .' Charlie's eyes widen as he searches for something to say. 'I'm doing okay, thanks.'

'It's so nice that you could come back for Christmas.

Can't imagine what Christmas must be like in a place like that.'

Noticeable tension draws up around us. The grandparents are luckily all having a separate conversation on the other sofa, and Mum and Dad are absent from the room, but Uncle Ant and Aunt Jules, all our cousins and various miscellaneous relatives now have their full attention on Charlie. Charlie's hands curl into fists.

'Well, it all got decorated for Christmas,' he says. 'And a lot of it was really helpful.'

I hate the way people react when they learn Charlie spent a few weeks as an in-patient. As if it's the most horrific thing they've ever heard. It's because it automatically makes them think *mental asylum* and *crazy people*, instead of *treatment* and *recovery* and *learning to manage an eating disorder*.

Don't get me wrong – I've read online that psych

wards are not *always* great places, like if they've got shitty staff or they're underfunded. But the one Charlie went to helped him more than me and Mum and Dad were ever able to. He had a whole team of experts helping him understand his feelings and start working towards recovery, without the distraction and pressure of school.

In all honesty, going to one probably saved Charlie's life.

Unfortunately, by the time I've tried to figure out how to say all of this to Uncle Ant, he has continued spouting absolute garbage.

'Oh, I'm sure,' continues Uncle Ant. 'But you hear some horror stories, don't you? White walls and straitjackets and all.'

Aunt Jules laughs and whacks Uncle Ant playfully on the arm. 'Oh, come on now, Antonio, no mental hospitals are really like that.'

'Psychiatric ward,' I correct her.

She clears her throat. 'Yes.' She shoots a wide grin at Charlie. 'We're *all* very happy that Charlie's better and back with us, aren't we?'

'Absolutely,' says Uncle Ant.

That's the other thing they don't get. They think eating disorders and mental illnesses can just be *fixed* at the drop of a hat. They don't understand that it's a process. That it takes time and treatment and effort and bad days and good days.

'Thanks,' says Charlie, but he looks like he's about to throw up.

'And how are you, Tori?' asks Aunt Jules. 'How's sixth form going?'

I begin to recite the classic answer to this question ('It's fine/it's a lot harder than GCSEs/it's nice not to have to do P.E. any more'), and as I do Charlie gets up and leaves the room. I excuse myself and follow him at my earliest opportunity, trying not to hate Ant and Jules as much as I actually do. It baffles me sometimes that people can just say stuff like that. That people can just have no idea about things.

I wander down the hallway and go to enter the kitchen, but stop when I see Charlie and Mum inside, standing in front of each other as if they're having a sort of face-off.

'Do you want us to talk about it or do you not want us to talk about it? You're being very immature, Charlie.'

'How am I being immature?'

'You're acting like a baby who just wants everyone's attention all of the time.'

'I don't want people's attention, that's the f— that's the *problem*.'

Mum rips her washing-up gloves off her hands. 'Look, everyone's aware that this is a *difficult* Christmas

41

for you, but you could at least recognise that we're *trying our best.*'

'*Trying your best?* What d'you want, a fucking congratulations certificate?'

'*Language.*'

'Half the time you refuse to even acknowledge that I have a fucking mental illness, and the other half you try as hard as possible to make me feel like I'm the last person you ever wanted as a child!'

And that's when Mum snaps.

'*GET OUT!*' She points towards the kitchen door. 'Just . . . *get out.*'

Charlie doesn't say anything at all. He turns around, walks away, exits the room and finds me there. Mum disappears out of view and Charlie stands there, looking down at me.

'I'm going to Nick's,' he says, in what he tries to make a calm voice.

'Oh,' I say.

He turns around and starts putting his shoes on.

'Please don't,' I say.

'I can't . . .' He stands back up. 'I can't deal with –' he gestures towards the living room and the kitchen – 'all of that.'

'It's Christmas, though,' I say.

'Let's be honest,' he continues as if he hadn't heard me, 'I'm just the joke of the family, anyway.'

'You're not.'

He reaches into the porch and grabs his coat and a gift bag of presents for Nick. 'This winter's been the fucking worst.'

He picks up a spare key and opens the door. It's raining. The cold comes in.

I want to cry. I want to do anything to stop him from leaving.

'Can't you at least spend Christmas with me?' I say.

He turns back. His eyes are watery. 'What does that mean?'

'You spend all of your time with Nick anyway.'

He starts to shout at me. 'That's because he treats me as something other than fucking mentally ill!'

I stay quite still.

'I do too . . .' I say, but my voice trails off.

'Sorry,' he says, but he's already leaving. 'I'll see you later.'

The door closes and I don't move.

I look down at my grey skirt and I really wish I was wearing jeans. I don't feel like myself. I realise I still have my cracker crown on, so I take it off and tear it into several pieces.

I probably should have seen this coming.

He's being unfair, but I don't have any right to be annoyed at him.

I walk back into the kitchen. Mum is still washing

up. I walk up to her, and her face looks like stone. Like ice, maybe. There's a pause, and then she says, 'You know, I *am* trying my best.'

I know she is, but her best isn't really good enough, and it shouldn't be about how *she* feels anyway. I walk out of the kitchen and sit on the stairs.

Oliver runs past me with one of his new tractors.

I go into the porch and open the door to see whether Charlie is just sitting on the kerb at the end of our driveway. But he isn't. Winter is usually my favourite season, but Charlie's right – this winter has been the worst. I sit down in the porch, my feet sticking out of the doorframe. There are some fairy lights outside someone's house across the road, but the more I look at them, the dimmer they seem to get. It doesn't feel like Christmas.

I think I'm trying my best too. I sit with him at every mealtime. I ask him how he is every day and sometimes he tells me. I started being his friend as well as his sister.

Not that that matters. I don't matter. *He* matters.

A car drives past. It's getting sort of dark now. Dark and cold and rainy. I think about how nice that is, and then I laugh to myself. Since when did they become my favourite things?

Charlie Francis Spring,
Age 15

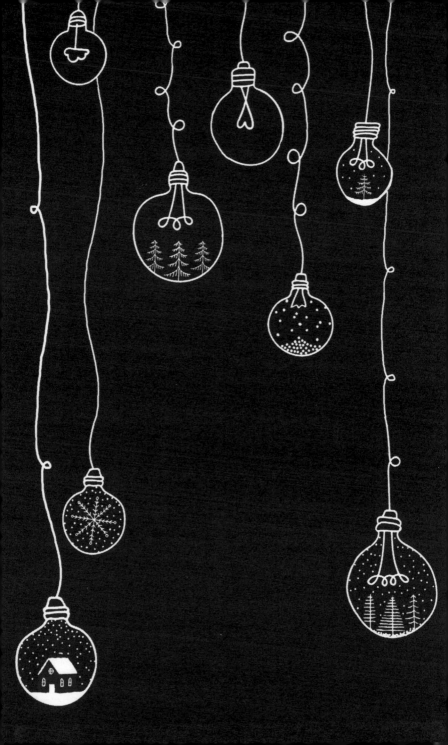

Charlie

Nick Nelson

(00:01) *Happy Christmas you xxxxxxxxxxxxx*

Charlie Spring

(00:02) *happy christmas xxxxxxxxxxxxxxxxxxxx*
i love you loads

Nick Nelson

(00:02) *Go to sleep you mug*

(00:03) *(I love you loads too xxxxxxxxxxxxxxx)*

Charlie Spring

(06:31) *oliver's waking victoria up with the musical xmas card i bought him hahahahahaha*

(06:32) *i don't know why i'm laughing, i'm awake too*

(06:32) *Oh how the tables turn*

Nick Nelson

(10:40) *HAHAHA.*

(10:40) *This has to be the latest I have ever woken up on Christmas Day.*

Charlie Spring

(13:23) *WHEN IS YOUR NEW PUPPY ARRIVING*

Nick Nelson

(13:30) *MY NAN JUST BROUGHT HIM ROUND!!!!!!!!!!!!!!!!!*

(13:30) *HE'S A PUG*

Charlie Spring

(13:31) *SCREAMING*

Nick Nelson

(13:32) *I'M DEAD*

(13:34)

Charlie Spring

(13:35) *unfair*

Nick Nelson

(13:36) *Another reason for you to come over later . . .*

Charlie Spring

(13:37) *the pug is now the only reason*

Nick Nelson

(13:38) *Stop texting me loser. Go be sociable.*

Charlie Spring

(13:38) *:-(*

Nick Nelson

(13:39) *<3*

Charlie Spring

(13:51) *a dog is for life*

(13:51) *not just for christmas*

Nick Nelson

(13:53) *Dog is life*

Charlie Spring

(13:54) *ball is life*

Nick Nelson

(13:55) *That's what Henry the Pug said*

Charlie Spring

(13:56) *you named him HENRY*

Nick Nelson

(13:57) *Yep!!!!*

Charlie Spring

(13:57) *that's a name for a train, not a dog*

Nick Nelson

(13:58) *Have you been watching Thomas the Tank Engine with Oliver again?*

Charlie Spring

(13:58) *maybe*

Nick Nelson

(13:59) *Nerd*

Charlie Spring

(13:59) *u love it*

Nick Nelson

(14:00) *Yes your interest in trains turns me on greatly*

Charlie Spring

(14:01) *screenshotted for future reference*

Nick Nelson

(14:02) *GO AND SOCIALISE YOU ABSOLUTE TRAIN NERD*

★

Charlie Spring

(15:14) *hey can i come over earlier than i said i would?*

Nick Nelson

(15:17) *Yeah of course, what's up?? You ok?*

Charlie Spring

(15:23) *yeah family's just being a bit annoying*

(15:24) *i'm the novelty gay mentally ill cousin*

Nick Nelson

(15:25) *Oh Char :-(you don't wanna just stick it out with Tori for a bit?*

Charlie Spring

(15:29) *she can't really do anything to help tbh*

(15:34) *i can just come over later if you're busy*

Nick Nelson

(15:35) *It's busy but jesus I could do with a break. Seriously it's fucking chaos in this house!!*

(15:36) *Mum's downed two bottles of Merlot and put the Michael Bublé Christmas album on. There are old people dancing in the lounge.*

(15:36) *Feel free to come over whenever, I need a break from the madness xxxx*

> **Charlie Spring**
>
> (15:37) *ok i'll leave in a bit xxxxxx*

> **Nick Nelson**
>
> (15:38) *You okay though? <3*

> **Charlie Spring**
>
> (15:39) *i'm fine <3*

I'm quite aware that it's my fault that my family are annoyed with me, so I guess the best way to sort that out is to just go away completely. I'm usually in favour of 'sorting things out' when I have a problem, but I think this is one of those things that I just can't fix. There've been a lot of things like that lately.

I also know I'm a hypocritical piece of shit. I complain all the time about people feeling sorry for me, but I still manage to be as dramatic as possible, running away to my boyfriend's house on Christmas Day, trying not to start crying and/or ruin Christmas for everyone. What the hell are people supposed to do when I act like this? Way to live up to my 'crazy person' stereotype.

I know Tori's trying her best to help. I feel kind of bad for running out on her like that. Out of everyone in my family, she's probably being the most genuinely helpful, and I seriously do appreciate her. She doesn't pester and she doesn't avoid the issue, which my parents are apparently pros at. I don't feel like a maniac when I'm talking to her.

Okay. Sorry. My therapist – Geoff – said I shouldn't call myself a 'maniac'. Or a 'crazy person'. Because I'm not. I know I'm not. I guess sometimes it feels good to exaggerate.

I *am* doing better. I'm not lying about that. I get that 'spending a few weeks in a psych ward' sounds like the most horrific thing ever to some people. I guess I've heard horror stories about some places that treat patients really badly. But for me, it was exactly what I needed. I got to start therapy properly. I got to meet other people my age who have eating disorders. I had a team of people assigned to help me start working towards recovery.

And it made me realise that my coping *mechanisms* – the restrictive eating, the self-harm, and my other compulsions – are just that: coping mechanisms. It's not about just stopping myself doing those things, it's about figuring out *why* I feel those impulses. What the emotional stuff is underneath.

While there'll be good days and bad days, I *can* get better.

God. Now I sound like Geoff.

And I think today is turning out to be one of the bad days.

Nick lives in a detached house a couple of streets away. He told me his family always have these giant Christmas parties with like a hundred people, and he wasn't joking. The front door is open, people's voices echo from every window, there are flashing lights coming from the living room, and I can feel the bass vibrations through my feet. It's a wonder they haven't been reported by their neighbours.

Since this is our first Christmas as a couple, I was going to drop in for an hour in the evening anyway once most of my relatives had entered a wine-induced slumber, but now here I am at only 4pm.

Charlie Spring

(16:02) i'm outside! xxxx

I stand and wait on their doorstep. Just walking into

the house would probably be a bit awkward, and I doubt anyone would hear the doorbell if I tried to ring it. Luckily, Nick quickly appears at the doorway.

He looks at me for a couple of seconds, and then folds his arms. 'You didn't bring an umbrella?'

I glance up at the sky. I hadn't even noticed it was raining, but when I look down at myself, I realise that my clothes are completely soaked.

'Oh,' I say, and look back at him.

'Hey,' he says with a grin.

Since me and Nick got together in April, a lot of shit has gone down. But despite it all – the ED voice getting louder in the summer, the self-harm relapse in the autumn – Nick has stuck by me and tried to support me however he can.

At first, I was scared to tell him about all of my mental health stuff. I thought he might not want to date me any more if he knew. But, in actual fact, opening up about that stuff made us stronger as a couple.

I know a lot of people think teenage relationships don't last, or they're not as 'deep' as adult relationships, but me and Nick? I think we've got something different.

Something great.

'Hi,' I say and step inside.

He shuts the door and turns to face me, his grin gone. He brushes some of my drenched hair out of my eyes. 'You look like shit, Charles.'

I let my forehead fall on to his shoulder. 'Yup.' His arms wrap around me instantly and I lift mine to hold him too, and he rests his head against mine and his hair brushes my ear and he pulls me against him.

We stay like that, in the cold porch, just for a few minutes, without saying anything, without moving, and then he whispers, 'You okay?' and I start to cry, because

that's always what happens when people ask me that question. I really don't want him to see me cry, because there's been far too much of that recently and it's Christmas Day, so I try extremely hard not to move from his shoulder, but that doesn't stop him seeing. When he pulls back, the tears are streaming down my face.

'Sorry, I just. . . just had an argument with my mum,' I say, trying to sound fine but obviously not succeeding.

Nick looks at me for a moment, concerned. Then he removes a handkerchief from the back pocket of his trousers. The sheer ridiculousness of Nick owning a handkerchief immediately makes me snort out a laugh, which makes him smile too and raise his eyebrows, and I do stop crying as he methodically wipes my cheeks.

'Why do you have a handkerchief?' I ask.

Nick breaks out into a grin, still gently brushing

the thing against my face. 'Owning a handkerchief is cool now.'

'Oh. I haven't been keeping up with current trends.'

Nick laughs. It's so lovely against the sound of the rain and the low bass of whatever music they're playing in the living room. 'Okay, *maybe* it was a Christmas present that I put in my pocket just to prove to my nan that I would actually use it.' He puts it back into his pocket and then takes my face in both of his hands. 'And what d'you know? I *did* use it.'

I smile at him, his hands feeling so warm against my skin. 'Maybe your nan knows me better than you do.'

'Are you suggesting that you want to date my nan?'

'There are so many reasons why I do not want to do that.'

'Good.' He hugs me again, his arms reaching round my waist. 'Thought I had some competition for a minute there.'

'You don't have any competition,' I say, running my hands up to his shoulders, wanting to just stay here forever with him in the porch, live here in the cold with the rain falling next to us, make a bed out of the coats and a fire out of the coat rack.

'You smooth little bastard,' he says, leaning in with a smile and I meet him with a kiss that turns into a longer kiss than either of us planned but everything is suddenly far too nice for it to end. I run a hand through his hair and he pulls my hips against his and our lips brush as he changes direction and, for a brief moment, it actually feels like Christmas.

'I assume this is the boyfriend, then?'

Nick and I jolt apart and turn to find that we've drawn an audience of at least seven family members of varying ages.

'Gonna introduce us, mate?' continues the guy who just spoke – possibly an uncle, or an older cousin.

'Oh, yeah,' Nick replies, still in a daze. He moves behind me and pushes me further into his house, with his hands on my shoulders, towards his family, who seem to be multiplying in numbers as more people walk through the hallway and realise that I've arrived. 'So this is Charlie.'

*

A good half an hour is spent introducing me to every single member of Nick's family, who for some reason all want to meet me. Everything is, 'Oh, so this is Charlie, then?' and nobody asks any awkward questions about hospital or how I found Christmas dinner or anything like that. Throughout most of this, I'm carrying the new Nelson family puppy, Henry, who is the tiniest and palest pug puppy I have ever seen. Henry falls asleep in my arms and I fall immediately in love with him.

Nick's other dog, a border collie named Nellie, trails along behind us, occasionally bopping her nose against my leg. I wish my parents let me have pets.

Nick's mum still has her cracker hat on and, even though I've seen her numerous times since I came home, she gives me a hug lasting at least ten seconds longer than is socially acceptable. I don't really mind, though.

After that, Nick drags me up to his room so I can

change clothes, despite my protests that I don't mind staying in my soaked jeans.

As I'm changing, Nick's lounging on his big double bed. He's wearing his usual old jeans, but with them he's got on this bright red jumper with reindeer patterns on it. It's disgusting and absolutely hilarious.

'I like your jumper,' I say, as I'm doing my belt up. 'It's very sexual.'

Nick looks down, as if he'd forgotten what he was wearing. 'Oh, yeah,' he says. 'I know, right.' He looks up at me and waggles his eyebrows. 'So seductive.'

I pick up my damp jeans from the floor, chuck them at his face, and laugh as he dramatically rolls off his bed in an attempt to catch them.

'I like *your* jumper,' he says, after crawling back on to his bed, a small smile playing on his lips. 'Whoever picked that out has proper taste.'

I'm momentarily confused and then realise I'm

wearing Nick's navy Adidas jumper. I 'borrowed' it a few months back and then 'forgot' to give it back.

Look, boyfriend jumpers are the best, okay? Big, comfy, and they smell good.

'Oh. Oops,' I say.

I inspect myself in the mirror. Nick's jeans, pretty much the same as mine, but several sizes larger, look ridiculous on me. I groan heavily.

'I look like a nineties boy-band member.'

Nick appears behind me. He's not actually that much taller than me, he's just *broader*. Which is great from, like, an aesthetic perspective. But not from a clothes-sharing perspective.

'Well, it's this or joggers, and I guarantee my mum will have something to say if you turn up to our Christmas party in joggers.'

'I think joggers would make me look even *more* like a member of the Backstreet Boys.'

'Nothing wrong with the Backstreet Boys.'

Nick meets my eye in the mirror. We stay silent for a moment, and then he takes my hand, so I turn to face him.

'You okay?' he says. 'D'you wanna talk about it?'

I know I probably should. I should explain about the argument with Mum and all the arguments we've had over the past few weeks. I should explain how difficult it is to keep trying to do better when there are so many people who just refuse to understand how hard it is. I should explain that I barely slept last night because I was so anxious about dinner and, even though I actually did quite well, I still felt like everyone was watching me, waiting for me to fuck up and ruin the day.

But it's so much easier to just not think about it.

'I just . . . wanted to have a nice day,' I say, and I feel myself welling up again.

'Okay,' he says, slinging an arm round my shoulders and walking me out of his room, then kissing me on the top of the head. 'Let's do that, then.'

★

'Oh, all right, Charlie?'

Half an hour later, Nick's gone to the loo and I'm suddenly facing David – Nick's older brother by four years – while I'm drinking a glass of water in the kitchen.

David's not really like Nick in any way except for their identical dark blond hair. David's a lot shorter – shorter than me, actually – and completely up himself. He goes to a posh university and hangs out with lots of private-school guys who do rowing and wear quilted jackets. He has been known to boast about cheating on his girlfriends.

Nick and David don't really like each other and I don't think David likes me very much, either. When

Nick came out to him as bisexual, David laughed and told him he was just covering up being gay.

'Hey,' I say.

He grabs a beer bottle from the fridge. It's definitely not his first.

'So you all cured and stuff, man?' he says.

'Er . . .' This is possibly the most ridiculous question I've received all day. 'Well, that's not really how it works, but I'm doing better, thanks.'

'Oh, ace.' He takes a swig of beer and stares at me like I'm a zoo animal.

'How are you?' I ask, purely out of there not being anything else to say.

'Oh, I'm really good, thanks, yeah,' he says. 'Uni work, rowing, you know. Work hard, play hard, mate.'

'Cool.'

'So what's happening with you now? You allowed back at school yet?'

Allowed. Everything about him irritates me.

'I'm going back next term,' I say.

'Oh, nice, nice.' He takes another swig. 'So, like, I'm super interested – what's it like in a mental hospital? Did you meet anyone *really* crazy?'

I just stand there, silent.

''Cause, like,' he continues, 'I was watching this documentary on schizophrenia the other day and literally it's just fucking *awful*, innit? All that talking to yourself and stuff. And these people, they had to be locked up to stop them hurting themselves, you know?'

My grip on my glass tightens. I could just leave. 'Well, I don't have schizophrenia. And documentaries like that are designed to horrify you and sensationalise mental illness, particularly less "socially acceptable" illnesses like schizophrenia.'

David blinks. 'Oh, yeah, man, obviously. But you

must have met people like that, surely, in that place?'

'Well, actually the place I was at was mainly for people with eating disorders, so—'

'Just fucking *crazy*, innit. So fucking sad.'

'. . . Sure.'

'Must have been fucking awful to not want to eat anything as well, mate. Sounds crap.'

I don't say anything.

'Like, did you ever get so hungry that you just *had* to eat something? That's what I don't get, like, the people who just stop eating and *die*, you know?'

And then Nick walks into the room.

By the look on his face, he's obviously heard David's last comment, and it probably doesn't help that I shoot him a look of severe distress.

'Are you done interrogating my boyfriend, David?' he asks, not politely.

David frowns and holds out his hands. 'Mate, we were just having a chat!'

'D'you seriously think Charlie wants to listen to your fucking ignorant views on *Christmas Day*?' Nick snaps, and it's been a while since I've seen him get this angry. 'What the fuck?'

David snorts and takes a sip of beer. 'All right, all right, calm your tits.'

'Fucking hell.' Nick puts his arm around me and walks us out of the kitchen and down the hallway. Once we're out of earshot, he says, 'He's such an insensitive little prick.'

'It's fine.'

'It's *not*.'

Nick's right. It's not fine. I should have defended myself better.

I'm tired, though. I'm so tired of defending myself.

'Sorry,' I mumble. 'I should have . . . argued back.'

Nick shakes his head. 'No, it's him who should be sorry. You shouldn't have to argue with people about this.'

Nick leads us into the alcove by the garage door. His arm drops but his hands find mine.

I've talked to Geoff a lot about people like David. Unhelpful people.

When people know you're mentally ill, most people either want to ignore it completely or they treat you like you're strange, scary, or fascinating. Very few people are actually good at the middle ground.

The middle ground isn't hard. It's just *being there*. Being helpful, if help is needed. Being understanding, even if they don't understand everything.

'Thanks,' I say and kiss Nick gently.

Nick's good at the middle ground. My parents aren't, really, but I know they're trying and occasionally they succeed. And they're better at it than David, that's for sure.

Tori's good at the middle ground too. Maybe I was a bit harsh on her earlier.

Nick and I look at each other for a moment in the shade of the alcove.

'Today's been shit,' I say eventually, letting out a small laugh.

Nick smiles sadly. 'Yeah, I got that impression.' He squeezes my hands. 'Wanna talk about it?'

I pause to think. 'Maybe a bit later?'

He squeezes my hands again. 'Yeah. Of course.'

'Can we go cuddle Henry? I feel like I'm missing out on valuable puppy appreciation time.'

Nick grins. 'An excellent idea.'

★

When Nick said it was chaos in his house, he meant it. After some dog playtime with Henry and Nellie, we find a proper disco going on in the living room and a rather enthusiastic game of toy-car racing happening in the hallway with people's shoes as obstacles. After I beat Nick five times at that, we somehow get dragged into a game of Monopoly, which is promptly ruined when Henry gallops over the board, followed by a Mario Kart tournament with Nick's older cousins, which I also win. Apparently I'm good at driving games.

Then we go back to Nick's room to exchange presents. I got him a bunch of things he likes – a grid-paper notebook and a fountain pen, a fish-eye lens that attaches to his phone, and a giant Oreo Dairy Milk bar. Nick got me some fancy headphones – way fancier than my current ones that are broken in one ear. And we also got each other the most stupidly romantic cards ever – his has pictures of us all over it and I drew all over mine.

I kiss him after I read his card and he kisses me back and basically we end up making out for like half an hour.

And suddenly it's seven o'clock and we're sitting on a living room sofa with *Doctor Who* on in the background, my legs resting over his and his head on my shoulder. Some kids are sitting on the carpet building a Lego pirate ship and Nick's mum and various aunts and uncles are busy organising the buffet tea on the dining table.

I'm about to fall asleep when I hear Nick's voice.

'Char, just so you know, your phone has been making sounds for the past five minutes.'

'Oh.' I sit up a little and Nick does too, a sleepy smile on his face. I withdraw my phone from my pocket to find the screen covered in unread texts.

The messages are all from Tori. Nick leans in to read them too.

Victoria Spring

(17:14) Hey when are you coming home?

(17:32) Please reply to me

(17:40) At least just tell me when you're coming home

(17:45) Mum and Dad are kind of upset I don't think they're gonna shout at you

(18:03) I think Mum's sorry tbh

(18:17) Oliver wants to know when you're coming home, he wants to play Mario Kart

(18:31) Can't believe you left me alone with Clara you fucking twat

(18:54) If you don't reply soon I'm literally gonna walk to Nick's and get you

(18:59) I'm not even joking

(19:00) Charlie

(19:01) Charlie

(19:01) Charlie

(19:01) Seriously

Nick doesn't say anything, but I can tell he wants to. I instantly feel like shit.

I've had a bad day, sure. But I shouldn't have taken that out on Tori.

I should have stuck with her for at least a little longer.

'I should probably go home,' I say.

Nick runs his fingers through my hair. I'm pretty sure he doesn't want me to go home, but he still says, 'Yeah.'

Neither of us make any sign of moving.

He looks at me with his big brown eyes and he doesn't have to say anything. I know he wants me to open up to him. To just get it all out.

'Today's just been really hard,' I begin, and Nick takes my hand while I tell him everything. I tell him about the arguments. About the stress and the sleeplessness and all my annoying relatives. About how I just wanted to have a 'normal' Christmas Day, whatever that is.

I know Nick can't fix anything. Even if he could, he shouldn't have to. But just talking about everything eases a bit of the tightness in my chest.

'I guess . . . a part of me wanted to pretend that this Christmas could just be the same as last Christmas,' I say. I can't quite meet his eyes. 'If I just pretended nothing was different. But everyone was just doing the absolute most to make me feel like a liability.'

'Everyone?' Nick asks.

'Maybe except Tori. She's the only one who's all right. Like, she's helpful but she also just talks to me like normal.' I huff out a laugh. 'Well, Oliver too, I guess.'

Nick wraps one arm around me. I snuggle on to his shoulder.

'It sounds like your mum and dad sort of wanted to pretend that this Christmas could be "normal" too,' he says.

I nod. 'Yeah. That's exactly it.'

'Have you talked to them about it?'

'About what?'

'Like . . . did you explain that this Christmas would be different and you might need a bit of extra support?'

I think back. Me and Dad agreed on a meal plan for the day, but apart from that . . .

'Not really,' I mumble.

'I think sometimes,' says Nick, 'you're so scared of being a burden that it makes you terrified to ask for help. But you have lots of people around you that would be there for you, if you opened up about what help you need.'

I look up at him. I love him. God, I love my boyfriend.

'Now you sound like Geoff,' I say, grinning, and he laughs and gives me a little shove.

And then I realise that my sister is standing in the living-room doorway.

Tori obviously forgot to bring an umbrella too – she looks like she just jumped into a river. She's also quite out of breath, meaning she probably jogged here, and she looks angry in that completely silent way of hers – death-stare eyes, lips clenched together, fists dug into her coat pockets.

'Firstly,' she says, 'Nick, I refuse to believe that you have this many family members. It's not logical. Secondly, your disgusting brother tried to flirt with me again and I swear to God if he doesn't get the message soon I'm going to find a fucking well and push him into it.'

All of the kids building the Lego pirate ship turn around in shock. Tori looks at them and raises her eyebrows menacingly. They quickly turn away again.

Nick laughs heartily but Tori's face doesn't change. She looks at me.

'Thirdly, I think you should come home now,

because if I have to answer one more bloody question about my school grades I might do a runner as well and Dad's already really upset as it is.' She moves her weight to her other leg. 'Also, Oliver's in a bad mood because no one will play Mario Kart with him, and Grandma wants to talk to you about your drumming lessons, *and* I think Mum might actually be willing to *apologise*, as wild as that sounds.'

She slumps into the other end of the sofa, not looking at us, and tilts her head back into the cushions.

I have no idea what to say.

I move away from Nick and sit next to her. I put my arms around her and, after a few seconds, she leans on my shoulder.

'I hate Christmas,' she says.

'No you don't,' I say.

'I hate this one.'

'Everyone hates this one. This whole winter's been a bit shit.'

'Yup.'

Doctor Who still plays on in the background. Oliver's probably watching it right now.

'Sorry I ran out,' I say. 'Thank you for coming to get me.'

She looks at me. 'Sorry today was shit for you.'

'It's not been all bad. Nick's got a new puppy.'

Tori snorts. 'Can you two just get married, buy a house, and get three dogs already?'

Me and Nick laugh, and then the three of us sit in silence for a moment. I rest my temple on Tori's hair.

'I'm going to try harder to say when I need help,' I say. 'And explain how I need help.'

'Is that what Geoff told you to do?'

'Yeah, but then Nick said it as well and I think they're both right.'

'Good,' says Tori, her voice a little softer. 'I think . . . that would be good.'

It won't fix anything. I know that.

But maybe this whole 'recovery' thing could be a little easier if I reached out to people every now and then.

'You missed Grandad and Abuelo's annual argument,' Tori says, after a while.

'What was it about this year?'

'I think it was about antique furniture, but most of Abuelo's points were in Spanish and that's not my area. I needed you to commentate.'

'There might be another round later, like last year.'

'Hopefully. It at least stopped Clara trying to get me to describe my ideal man.'

I laugh, and then she laughs too, and everything's a little bit better. Just for a minute or so.

Oliver Jonathan Spring,
Age 7

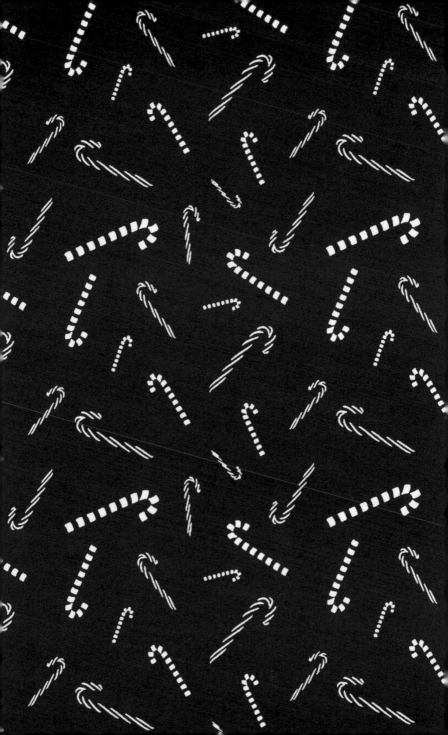

Oliver

First Charlie disappeared, and then Tori disappeared, and I'm starting to wonder whether I'm next. Nobody seems to be saying anything about it, which makes me wonder whether my family are behind it, and they've all been possessed by some ghosts or evil dinosaurs or something. I'm playing Mario Kart right now in front of the TV to take my mind off it, but that doesn't mean that I'm not very worried.

Mario Kart's kind of boring when you play it by yourself.

Rosanna keeps touching my hair and it's really annoying me.

Mum comes up to me just as I've finished Luigi Circuit and asks if I need another drink. I shake my head and ask, 'Where's Charlie and Tori?'

Mum sits down on the sofa to my right. She's got a glass of wine in one hand. 'They've just gone out for a little bit.'

'Have they been kidnapped?'

'No, oh, darling, no.'

'Where've they gone?'

Mum doesn't say anything for a little bit. Maybe she doesn't know ...

'Charlie was a bit upset earlier, so he went to Nick's house.'

Nick is Charlie's boyfriend, who comes round our house all the time. I think they'll probably get married one day so they can have their own house and not have to walk to each other's houses every single day.

I put down the controller. Charlie's been upset quite a lot lately because he has a mental illness. But Mum says he's getting better because he has to talk about his feelings to a special doctor called Geoff. Geoff sounds cool.

'Is it because of his mental illness?'

'. . . Sort of, yes.'

'Oh. Is he going to get better soon?'

Mum sips her wine. 'It's complicated, sweetheart. It takes time. But I hope so.'

'Where's Tori?'

'I think she's gone to see if Charlie wants to come home yet.'

'Oh.'

'I said some . . . not very nice things,' Mum says, and rests her chin in one hand, 'to Charlie.'

I suddenly realise that she looks really sad. Mum's never ever sad about things – she gets angry sometimes and complains when I leave all my tractors on the lounge windowsill or make too much noise in the car, but she doesn't really get sad.

I get up off the floor and go and give her a hug, which is what you have to do when someone is sad.

She laughs and pats me on the head. 'Aw, Oliver. I'm okay.'

'You could just say sorry,' I say. 'That's what you have to do when you say something bad. Say sorry.'

'You're completely right,' she says, and when I step back, she's smiling, so I must have done a good job with the hug.

And then I hear the front door open.

I immediately run out of the lounge and down the hallway and there, taking their shoes off, are my big brother and sister, soaked from the rain. I run towards Charlie because he's the only one left in my family who still picks me up and, when he sees me, he grins and holds out his arms and lifts me into the air and says, 'Cor, you're getting so

heavy. You're like an elephant, you are.'

'No I'm *not*.'

Tori ruffles my hair, which isn't as annoying as when Rosanna does it. 'What age are you going to stop being carried everywhere?'

I take a moment to consider. 'Twenty-seven.'

They both laugh and Charlie carries me into the lounge, Tori following us. When we get there, Charlie puts me down and then he goes and gives Mum a hug, which is nice, because hugs always make everything better.

Then they go into the kitchen. I can hear them talking, but I'm not sure what they're saying. Hopefully Mum's saying sorry, like I told her to.

Tori sits on the other sofa and I sit next to her and say, 'Everything's better when all three of us are here.'

Tori looks at me. 'Definitely.'

'Why did you go away? I was so *bored*. This

Christmas has been so boring.'

She looks at me some more. 'Well . . . it's been something.'

I don't really know what that means.

'But I promise we won't go away ever again,' she says.

'You can't promise that,' I say. 'You have to go to school.'

'Okay, next time we go somewhere, we'll tell you before we go.'

'Fine. *And* you have to promise to come back.'

Tori smiles. 'Okay. We'll definitely promise to come back.'

'Good.'

Being on my own without a brother or a sister would be weird. I don't think I'd like it. Who are you supposed to play with or ask to reach stuff for you? There wouldn't be anyone to carry me around. And there'd be two empty bedrooms in

the house and we'd probably get ghosts living here.
I really don't like ghosts.

'Can we play Mario Kart now?' I ask.

'Yes.' Tori ruffles my hair again. 'Yes, we can play
Mario Kart now.'

Further Resources

For information, help, support and guidance about mental health and mental illness, please check out the following resources:

Beat Eating Disorders
www.beateatingdisorders.org.uk/

YoungMinds
www.youngminds.org.uk/

MindOut LGBTQ Mental Health Service
www.mindout.org.uk/

Rethink Mental Illness
www.rethink.org/

Switchboard LGBT+ Helpline
https://switchboard.lgbt/

Read an extract
from Alice's
debut novel . . .

Solitaire

'And your defect is a propensity to hate everybody.'

'And yours,' he replied with a smile, 'is wilfully to misunderstand them.'

Pride and Prejudice, Jane Austen

One

I am aware as I step into the common room that the majority of people here are almost dead, including me. I have been reliably informed that post-Christmas blues are entirely normal and that we should expect to feel somewhat numb after the 'happiest' time of the year, but I don't feel so different now to how I felt on Christmas Eve, or on Christmas Day, or on any other day since the Christmas holidays started. I'm back now and it's another year. Nothing is going to happen.

I stand there. Becky and I look at each other.

'Tori,' says Becky, 'you look a little bit like you want to kill yourself.'

She and the rest of Our Lot have sprawled themselves over a collection of revolving chairs around the common-room computer desks. As it's the first day back, there has been a widespread hair-and-make-up effort across the entire sixth form and I immediately feel inadequate.

I deflate into a chair and nod philosophically. 'It's funny because it's true.'

She looks at me some more, but doesn't really look, and we laugh at something that wasn't funny. Becky then realises that I am in no mood to do anything so she moves away. I lean into my arms and fall half asleep.

My name is Victoria Spring. I think you should know that I make up a lot of stuff in my head and then get sad about it. I like to sleep and I like to blog. I am going to die someday.

Rebecca Allen is probably my only real friend at the moment. She is also probably my best friend. I am as yet unsure whether these two facts are related. In any case, Becky Allen has very long purple hair. It has come to my attention that, if you have purple hair, people often look at you, thus resulting in you becoming a widely recognised and outstandingly popular figure in adolescent society, the sort of figure that everyone claims to know yet probably hasn't even spoken to. She has a lot of Instagram followers.

Right now, Becky's talking to this other girl from Our Lot, Evelyn Foley. Evelyn is considered 'alternative' because she has messy hair and wears cool necklaces.

'The real question though,' says Evelyn, 'is whether there's sexual tension between Harry and Malfoy.'

I'm not sure whether Becky genuinely likes Evelyn.

Sometimes I think people only pretend to like each other.

'Only in fan fictions, Evelyn,' says Becky. 'Please keep your fantasies between yourself and your search history.'

Evelyn laughs. 'I'm just saying. Malfoy helps Harry in the end, right? So why does he bully Harry for seven years? He secretly likes him!' With each word, she claps her hands together. It really doesn't emphasise her point. 'It's a well-established fact that people tease people they fancy. The psychology here is unarguable.'

'Evelyn,' says Becky. 'Firstly, I resent the fangirl idea that Draco Malfoy is some kind of beautifully tortured soul who is searching for redemption and understanding. He's essentially a massive racist. Secondly, the idea that bullying means that you fancy someone is basically the foundation of domestic abuse.'

Evelyn appears to be deeply offended. 'It's just a book. It's not real life.'

Becky sighs and turns to me, and so does Evelyn. I deduce that I am under pressure to contribute something.

'I think Harry Potter's a bit shit, to be honest,' I say. 'Sort of wish we could all move on from it.'

Becky and Evelyn just look at me. I get the impression that I've ruined this conversation so I mumble an excuse and lift myself off my chair and hurry out of the common-room door. Sometimes I hate people. This is probably very bad for my mental health.

★

There are two grammar schools in our town: Harvey Greene Grammar School for Girls, or 'Higgs' as it is popularly known, and Truham Grammar School for Boys. Both schools, however, accept all genders in

Years 12 and 13, the two final years of school known countrywide as the sixth form. So, now that I am in Year 12, I have had to face a sudden influx of guys. Boys at Higgs are on a par with mythical creatures and having an actual real boyfriend puts you at the head of the social hierarchy, but personally, thinking or talking too much about 'boy issues' makes me want to shoot myself in the face.

Even if I did care about that stuff, it's not like we get to show off, thanks to our stunning school uniform. Usually, sixth-formers don't have to wear school uniform; however, Higgs sixth form are forced to wear a hideous one. Grey is the theme, which is fitting for such a dull place.

I arrive at my locker to find a pink Post-it note on its door. On that, someone has drawn a left-pointing arrow, suggesting that I should, perhaps, look in that direction. Irritated, I turn my head to the left. There's another Post-it note a few lockers along. And, on the wall at the end of the corridor, another. People are walking past them, totally oblivious. I guess people aren't observant. That, or they just don't care. I can relate to that.

I pluck the Post-it from my locker and wander to the next.

Sometimes I like to fill my days with little things that other people don't care about. It makes me feel like I'm doing something important, mainly because no one else is doing it.

This is one of those times.

The Post-its start popping up all over the place. The penultimate Post-it I find depicts an arrow pointing forwards and is situated on the door of a closed computer room on the first floor. Black fabric covers the door window. This particular computer room, C16, was closed last year for refurbishment, but it doesn't look like anyone's bothered getting started. It sort of makes me feel sad, to tell you the truth, but I open C16's door anyway, enter and close it behind me.

There's one long window stretching the length of the far wall, and the computers in here are bricks. Solid cubes. Apparently, I've time-travelled to the 1990s.

I find the final Post-it note on the back wall, bearing a URL:

SOLITAIRE.CO.UK

Solitaire is a card game you play by yourself. It's what I used to spend my IT lessons doing and it probably did a lot more for my intelligence than actually paying attention.

It's then that someone opens the door.

'Dear God, the age of the computers in here must be a criminal offence.'

I turn slowly around.

A boy stands before the closed door.

'I can hear the haunting symphony of dial-up connection,' he says, eyes drifting, and, after several long seconds, he finally notices that he's not the only person in the room.

He's a very ordinary-looking, not ugly but not hot, miscellaneous boy. His most noticeable feature is a pair of large, thick-framed square glasses that sort of make him look like he's wearing 3D cinema glasses. He's tall and has a side parting. In one hand, he holds a mug; in the other a piece of paper and his school planner.

As he absorbs my face, his eyes flare up and I swear to God they double in size. He leaps towards me like a pouncing lion, fiercely enough that I stumble backwards in fear that he might crush me completely. He leans forward so that his face is centimetres from my own. Through my reflection in his ridiculously oversized spectacles, I notice that he has one blue eye and one green eye. Heterochromia.

He grins violently.

'Victoria Spring!' he cries, raising his arms into the air.

I say and do nothing. I have a headache.

'You are Victoria Spring,' he says. He holds the piece of paper up to my face. It's a photograph. Of me. Underneath, in tiny letters: Victoria Spring, 11A. It has been on display near the staffroom – in Year 11, I was a form leader, mostly because no one else wanted to do it so I got volunteered. All the form leaders had their pictures taken. Mine is awful. It's before I cut my hair so I sort of look like the girl from *The Ring*. It's like I don't even have a face.

I look into the blue eye. 'Did you tear that right off the display?'

He steps back a little, retreating from his invasion of

my personal space. He's got this insane smile on his face. 'I said I'd help someone look for you.' He taps his chin with his planner. 'Blond guy . . . skinny trousers . . . walking around like he didn't really know where he was . . .'

I do not know any guys and certainly not any blond guys who wear skinny trousers.

I shrug. 'How did you know I was in here?'

He shrugs too. 'I didn't. I came in because of the arrow on the door. I thought it looked quite mysterious. And here you are! What a hilarious twist of fate!'

He takes a sip of his drink.

'I've seen you before,' he says, still smiling.

I find myself squinting at his face. Surely I must have seen him at some point in the corridors. Surely I would remember those hideous glasses. 'I don't think I've ever seen you before.'

'That's not surprising,' he says. 'I'm in Year 13, so you

wouldn't see me much. And I only joined your school last September. I did my Year 12 at Truham.'

That explains it. Four months isn't enough time for me to commit a face to memory.

'So,' he says, tapping his mug. 'What's going on here?'

I step aside and point unenthusiastically to the Post-it on the back wall. He reaches up and peels it off.

'Solitaire.co.uk. Interesting. Okay. I'd say we could boot up one of these computers and check it out, but we'd probably both expire before Internet Explorer loaded. I bet you any money they all use Windows 95.'

He sits down on one of the swivel chairs and stares out of the window at the suburban landscape. Everything is lit up like it's on fire. You can see right over the town and into the countryside. He notices me looking too.

'It's like it's pulling you out, isn't it?' he says. He

sighs to himself. 'I saw this old man on my way in this morning. He was sitting at a bus stop with headphones on, tapping his hands on his knees, looking at the sky. How often do you see that? An old man with headphones on. I wonder what he was listening to. You'd think it would be classical, but it could have been anything. I wonder if it was sad music.' He lifts up his feet and crosses them on top of a table. 'I hope it wasn't.'

'Sad music is okay,' I say, 'in moderation.'

He swivels round to me and straightens his tie.

'You are definitely Victoria Spring, aren't you.' This should be a question, but he says it like he's already known for a long time.

'Tori,' I say, intentionally monotone. 'My name is Tori.'

He puts his hands in his blazer pockets. I fold my arms.

'Have you been in here before?' he asks.

'No.'

He nods. 'Interesting.'

I widen my eyes and shake my head at him. 'What?'

'What what?'

'What's interesting?' I don't think I could sound less interested.

'We both came looking for the same thing.'

'And what is that?'

'An answer.'

I raise my eyebrows. He gazes at me through his glasses. 'Aren't mysteries fun?' he says. 'Don't you wonder?'

It's then that I realise that I probably don't. I realise that I could walk out of here and literally not give a crap about solitaire.co.uk or this annoying, loud-mouthed guy ever again.

But because I want him to stop being so goddamn patronising, I swiftly remove my phone from my blazer pocket, type solitaire.co.uk into the Internet address bar and open up the web page.

What appears almost makes me laugh – it's an empty blog. A troll blog, I guess.

What a pointless, pointless day this is.

I thrust the phone into his face. 'Mystery solved, Sherlock.'

At first, he keeps on grinning, like I'm joking, but soon his eyes focus downwards on to the phone screen and, in a kind of stunned disbelief, he removes the phone from my hand.

'It's . . . an empty blog . . .' he says, not to me but to himself, and suddenly (and I don't know how this happens) I feel deeply, deeply sorry for him. Because he looks so bloody sad. He shakes his head and hands my phone back to me. I don't really know what to do. He literally looks like someone's just died.

'Well, er . . .' I shuffle my feet. 'I'm going to form now.'

'No, no, wait!' He jumps up so we're facing each other.

There is a significantly awkward pause.

He studies me, squinting, then studies the photograph, then back to me, then back to the photo. 'You cut your hair!'

I bite my lip, holding back the sarcasm. 'Yes,' I say sincerely. 'Yes, I cut my hair.'

'It was so long.'

'Yes, it was.'

'Why did you cut it?'

I had gone shopping by myself at the end of the summer holidays because there was so much crap I needed for sixth form and Mum and Dad were busy and I just wanted it out of the way. What I'd failed to remember was that I am awful at shopping. My old school bag was ripped and dirty so I trailed through nice places – River Island and Zara and Urban Outfitters and Mango and Accessorize. But all the nice bags there were, like, fifty pounds, so that wasn't happening. Then I tried the cheaper places – New Look and Primark and H&M – but I couldn't find one I liked. I ended up going round all the shops selling bags a billion bloody times before having a slight breakdown on a bench by Costa Coffee in the middle of the shopping centre. I thought about starting Year 12 and all the things that I needed to do and all the new people that I might have to meet and all the people I would have to talk to and I caught a reflection of myself in a Waterstones window and I realised then that most of my face was covered up and who in the name of God would want to talk to me like that and I started to feel all of this hair on my forehead and my cheeks and how it plastered my shoulders and back and I felt it creeping around me like worms, choking me to death. I began to breathe very fast, so I went straight into the nearest hairdresser's and had it all cut to my shoulders and out of my face. The hairdresser didn't want to do it, but I was very insistent. I spent my school bag money on a haircut.

'I just wanted it shorter,' I say.

He steps closer. I shuffle backwards.

'You,' he says, 'do not say anything you mean, do you?'

I laugh again. It's a pathetic sort of expulsion of air, but for me that qualifies as a laugh. 'Who are you?'

He freezes, leans back, opens out his arms as if he's the Second Coming of Christ and announces in a deep and echoing voice: 'My name is Michael Holden.'

Michael Holden.

'And who are you, Victoria Spring?'

I can't think of anything to say because that is what my answer would be really. Nothing. I am a vacuum. I am a void. I am nothing.

Mr Kent's voice blares abruptly from the tannoy. I

turn round and look up at the speaker as his voice resonates down.

'All sixth-formers should make their way to the common room for a short sixth-form meeting.'

When I turn back round, the room is empty. I'm glued to the carpet. I open my hand and find the SOLITAIRE.CO.UK Post-it inside it. I don't know at what point the Post-it made its way from Michael Holden's hand to my own, but there it is.

And this, I suppose, is it.

This is probably how it starts.

The story continues
in Solitaire . . .

Solitaire

'The Catcher in the Rye for the digital age' – The Times

This is not a love story.

Solitaire
Alice Oseman

My name is Tori Spring. I like to sleep and I like to blog. Last year – before all that stuff with Charlie and before I had to face the harsh realities of A-Levels and university applications and the fact that one day I really will have to start talking to people – I had friends. Things were very different, I guess, but that's all over now.

Radio Silence

Frances has always been a study machine with one goal, elite university. Nothing will stand in her way; not friends, not a guilty secret – not even the person she is on the inside. But when Frances meets Aled, the shy genius behind her favourite podcast, she discovers a new freedom. He unlocks the door to Real Frances and for the first time she experiences true friendship, unafraid to be herself.

I Was Born for This

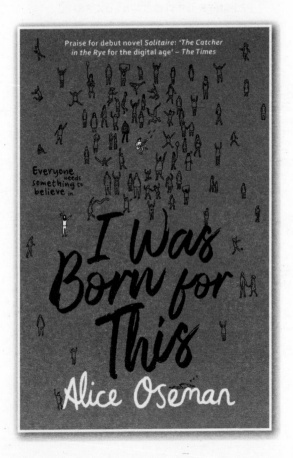

For Angel Rahimi life is about one thing: The Ark – a pop-rock trio
of teenage boys who are taking the world by storm. Being part of The
Ark's fandom has given her everything she loves – her friend Juliet,
her dreams, her place in the world. Jimmy Kaga-Ricci owes everything
to The Ark. He's their frontman – and playing in a band with his mates
is all he ever dreamed of doing.

Loveless

WINNER OF THE YA BOOK PRIZE

Praise for debut novel *Solitaire*: 'The Catcher in the Rye for the digital age' – *The Times*

Loveless

Alice Oseman

Georgia feels loveless – in the romantic sense, anyway. She's eighteen, never been in a relationship, or even had a crush on a single person in her whole life. She thinks she's an anomaly, people call her weird, and she feels a little broken. But she still adores romance – weddings, fan fiction, and happily-ever-afters. She knows she'll find her person one day . . . right?

Nick and Charlie

Everyone knows that Nick and Charlie are the perfect couple – that they're inseparable. But now Nick is leaving for university, and Charlie will be left behind at sixth form. But as the time to say goodbye gets inevitably closer, both Nick and Charlie question whether their love is strong enough to survive being apart. Or are they delaying the inevitable? Because everyone knows that first loves rarely last forever . . .

Out now in paperback

Heartstopper

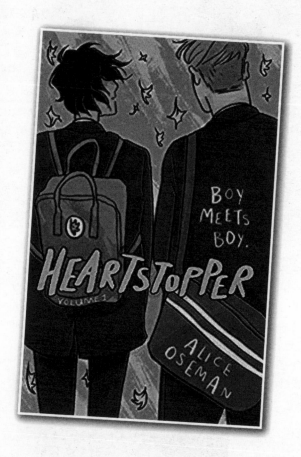

Boy meets boy. Boys become friends.
Boys fall in love. An LGBTQ+ graphic novel about life, love
and everything that happens in between – for fans of *The Art of
Being Normal*, Holly Bourne and *Love, Simon*.

Dear Santa,
I would like
the new
Mario kart
and a
tractor.
Love from
Oliver Spring

About Alice Oseman

Alice Oseman was born in 1994 in Kent, England. She completed a degree in English at Durham University in 2016 and is currently a full-time writer and illustrator. Alice can usually be found staring aimlessly at computer screens, questioning the meaninglessness of existence, or doing anything and everything to avoid getting an office job. Alice's first book, SOLITAIRE, was published when she was nineteen.

Follow Alice Oseman on Twitter and Instagram (@AliceOseman)